What Can I Give Jesus?

A Christmas Message for All Ages

CHERYL KIRKING

Illustrated By Ann Thomas

MILL HOUSE PRESS

Dedicated to David, Sarah Jean, Blake and Bryce. You are precious gifts!
And dedicated to you, the reader--may the Light of Christmas shine brightly in your heart.

To contact Cheryl Kirking for speaking events, concerts or to learn about her music and books, visit www.cherylkirking.com.

Book cover and internal design by Tressa Foster of Fresh Concepts (www.fresh-concepts.com)

Printed in China

Printed by Pettit Network, Inc.

First Edition—2007

Library of Congress Control Number: 2005932223

What can I give Jesus?/by Cheryl Kirking; illustrated by Ann Thomas

Summary: A young girl asks her mother what to give Jesus for his birthday and learns that by caring for others we give the best gift of all.

ISBN 0-9768847-1-2

ISBN 978-0-9768847-1-2

   [1.Christmas. 2.Christian Life—Juvenile Literature. 3. Christmas—Juvenile Literature.]

Given To

_____

From

_____

Date

_____

The house was finally quiet.

$\mathcal{T}$he kids were all in bed,

wrap presents
~~groceries~~
~~make coffee cake~~
~~frost cookies~~
~~mop floor~~
iron table cloth
polish silver
dust downstairs
vacuum

to:
from:

$\mathcal{A}$nd all the things I had to do
were running through my head.

I was putting one last package
beneath the tree and then

I heard my little daughter's voice,
"Mommy, tuck me in again."

I put her in her little bed
　　and tucked in her sheets;
She looked at me with big, bright eyes
　　saying "Mommy, I can't sleep.
I've got presents for you and Daddy,
　　for Grandma and Uncle Jim
But tomorrow's Jesus' birthday,
　　and I've got no gift for Him."

"What can I give Jesus, Mommy?
　　Please help me to see
What would a King like Jesus want
　　from a little girl like me?
If I could only send it,
　　I'd mail a package right away,
But I have nothing to give Him
　　and tomorrow's Christmas day."

Her face was so solemn
    with a halo of soft curls,
And I saw Jesus in the eyes
    of my little baby girl.
In that tender moment
    I brushed her cheek and smiled,
So thankful I could see God
    through the sweet eyes of a child.

"What can I give Jesus, Mommy?
    Please help me to see
What would a King like Jesus want
    from a little girl like me?
If I could only send it
    I'd mail a package right away,
But I have nothing to give Him,
    and tomorrow's Christmas day."

You gave Jesus a gift this morning
when you put your toys away;
You give Him a present every time
you smile at me that way!

The picture you drew for Grandma
was a gift to Jesus, too—

For He's right here beside us,
and He sees all we do.

$\mathcal{W}$hat can you give Jesus?
Honey, you've helped me to see
What our Savior, our Jesus, wants
from girls like you and me.

$\mathcal{Y}$ou gave Christ a gift tonight
by helping me to see
The important part of Christmas
is inside you and me.

*T*he most important part of Christmas
is inside you and me.

God made his light shine in our hearts.
— 2 Corinthians 4:6

Be a light for other people.
— Matthew 5:16

And a little child shall lead them.

— Isaiah 11:6

A Note from the Author

God has shown you his grace in giving you each different gifts.
And you are like servants who are responsible for using God's gifts.
So be good servants and use your gifts to serve each other.

— I Peter 4:10

Did you ever think about the gifts God has given you? The verse above tells us that God has blessed each of us with our own unique gifts, and we are to use them to bless others.

Maybe you have the ability to really listen to someone who needs to be heard. Or offer a smile to someone who could use an extra bit of kindness. Or color a picture, or tie a shoe. Our gifts may seem simple, but simple gifts are often the most cherished. You are precious to God, and so are the gifts he has given you to share with others!

Just as a present is not meant to stay in its wrapping paper, our gifts our meant to be used! This holiday season, and all year through, may we each use our gifts in gratitude to our loving Creator, who gave us Jesus, the greatest gift of all.

Cheryl

"I first heard *What Can I Give Jesus?* played on WNWC radio at 7:20 one morning, three days before Christmas. What a wonderful song to wake up to! It brought tears to my eyes! With two little girls that I knew would love the song, I immediately called the station to find out how to get a copy in time for Christmas. Thank you for such a beautiful Christmas message."
—Valerie Axelson, Wisconsin

"When I first heard *What Can I Give Jesus?*, I couldn't wait to share its message with my children. After listening to the song, my 7-year old son said "Mom, I want to give away my new bike." Karl had just won a bicycle in a drawing at our supermarket, and wanted to give it to a child who didn't have one. He donated it to the Salvation Army, who made sure it was given to a child in time for Christmas. What an impact the song had on my young son's heart! I am so glad the song is now illustrated and presented in this beautiful book our family will treasure."
—Kitty Law, Illinois

"*What Can I Give Jesus?*—a young girl's Christmas Eve conversation with her mother about what to give Jesus for His birthday—may help remind all of us about the 'reason for the season.' There's undeniably something special at work in this recording and one that I'll return to again."
—Doug Trouten, review in Twin Cities Christian newspaper

"Every December as our family hangs a royal purple stocking for Jesus, we plan what we want to give to Him for His birthday. Reading and listening to *What Can I Give Jesus?* this year will be a wonderful new part of our Christmas tradition."
—Diane Diston, Indiana

"It has been my privilege to air *What Can I Give Jesus?* on my radio program. It not only brought back precious memories but also helped me to receive its timely message of seeing Christmas in a most unforgettable way, 'through the eyes of a child.'
—Jim Mertz, KGFT-Colorado Springs, Colorado

"This is the book I've been waiting for! Last December I played *What Can I Give Jesus?* for my second grade Sunday School class. The kids loved the song, and now I can share the book with the class this Christmas. Thank you! "
—Barb Connors, Virginia

"After hearing Cheryl Kirking in concert at our church several years ago, we bought four CDs for each of our grown children, which we gave them for Christmas. Before dinner, we played the song *What Can I Give Jesus?* Each family member then named one way they would "give to God" in the coming year. It was very meaningful and even our youngest two-year-old grandchild could be a part. Playing *What Can I Give Jesus?* has become an annual Christmas Eve tradition at our house."
—Chuck and Gina Rafel, Arizona

"Listeners who have already discovered Cheryl Kirking's music will be pleased to learn that her memorable Christmas song *What Can I Give Jesus?* is now presented in a book, beautifully illustrated by artist Ann Thomas. It includes the CD, making it a perfect way to share the song, or to remind yourself of the true meaning of Christmas. This lovely book will surely become a perennial Christmas favorite for many."
—Jenifer Scott-Mayes, review in *Mom-to-Mom*

If you have enjoyed *What Can I Give Jesus?*, or it has had an impact you'd like to share, we would love to hear from you. Please contact us at www.whatcanigiveJesus.com or write: Mill House Press, P.O. Box 525 Lake Mills, Wisconsin 53551.

About the Author

Cheryl Kirking is a songwriter, author and conference speaker who tickles the funny bones and tugs at the heart strings of audiences nationwide through her Ripples of Encouragement™ presentations. She is a frequent contributor to the best-selling *Chicken Soup for the Soul* series of books. The mother of triplets, she enjoys small town life in Wisconsin with her family. To write Cheryl or find out how to bring her to your group or event, or to order her books and CDs, visit her website at www.cherylkirking.com.

Other books by Cheryl Kirking include:
Crayons in the Dryer: Misadventures and Unexpected Blessings of Motherhood
Ripples of Joy: Stories of Hope and Encouragement to Share
All is Calm, All is Bright: True Stories of Christmas
Teacher, You're an A+

About the Illustrator

Artist Ann Thomas is known for her detailed images in colored pencil, pen and ink, acrylic and watercolor that are used in childrens' books, greeting cards and other print media. She is also widely recognized for her fine architectural style renderings of homes, businesses and landmark buildings. She exhibits her work at a number of art shows. Ann freelances out of her home studio in Milwaukee, Wisconsin. She may be contacted at: www.AnnThomasIllustration.com

About the Song

When asked to write a song for her church's Christmas Eve service, Cheryl Kirking hoped to reach the young children with a Christmas message they could understand, while touching the hearts of adults as well. The song evoked a strong emotional response from listeners that evening, and many asked Kirking to record it. By the next Christmas, *What Can I Give Jesus?* was being played on radio stations across the country and the song's popularity began to grow as listeners responded to its encouraging message. It was later re-recorded to include the voice of Kirking's daughter, Sarah Jean. The song is now paired with the heartwarming illustrations of artist Ann Thomas in this gift book, sharing its timeless message for all ages.

Mill House Press donates a portion of the proceeds from this book to the Salvation Army, whose traditional red kettles are an integral part of the Christmas scene. The "miracle" of Christmas is repeated over and over again through the joy of caring and sharing, as kettle donations provide Christmas dinners, clothing, toys, and basic necessities to aid children and families, the homeless, and others in need. All year long, the Salvation Army offers hunger, disaster and refugee relief, cooperating with local and international relief agencies to bring comfort to those in need. Thank you for your support through this book purchase.

If you would like additional copies of this book, contact your favorite bookstore or www.millhousepress.com.
Quantity discounts are available through Mill House Press by calling (800) 772-0460.